for Nadia

Bloomsbury Publishing, London, New Delhi, New York and Sydney
First published in Great Britain in 2015 by Bloomsbury Publishing Plc
50 Bedford Square, London, WC1B 3DP

Text & illustrations copyright © Yasmeen Ismail 2015
The moral right of the author/illustrator has been asserted

A CIP catalogue record of this book is available from the British Library

ISBN 978 1 4088 5699 4 (HB)   ISBN 978 1 4088 5700 7 (PB)   ISBN 978 1 4088 5848 6 (eBook)
Printed in China by Leo Paper Products, Heshan, Guangdong

1 3 5 7 9 10 8 6 4 2

www.bloomsbury.com

All papers used by Bloomsbury Publishing are natural, recyclable products made from wood grown in well-managed forests.
The manufacturing processes conform to the environmental regulations of the country of origin.

BLOOMSBURY is a registered trademark of Bloomsbury Publishing Plc

I'm a Girl!

Yasmeen Ismail

BLOOMSBURY

LONDON NEW DELHI NEW YORK SYDNEY

I'm **supposed** to be *nice* . . .

all **sugar** and **spice** . . .

but I'm **sweet** *and* **sour,**
not a little flower!

Just watch me go –
always *fast*, never **s l o w**.

I'm a girl ...

I'm a girl!

And I am as **brave** as anyone else I know.

I like to be **spontaneous**
and do things my **own** way.
When I do, it's **much more FUN!**

I want to learn **everything** – I'd like to know the **lot**.
My brain is **FULL** of 'knowing things'.

I think I'm rather **musical**.
I have **rhythm** and an ear
for **melody**.

I'm a girl!

Uff!
Boys are
so noisy!

I'm a girl!

I like to play games – **all sorts** of games.
There's no **right** or **wrong** way to
play when you play 'pretend'.

Dolls are for girls.

It's **OK** to want to be **good** at things.

I like to be the **BEST**.

I'm a...

boy!